P9-APZ-373

10|18

Thanksgiving

by Pearl Markovics

Consultant:
Beth Gambro
Reading Specialist
Yorkville, Illinois

Contents

BEARPORT
PUBLISHING

New York, New York

Thanksgiving

What day is it?

It is Thanksgiving!

It is Thanksgiving.

I see the table.

It is Thanksgiving.

I see the yams.

It is Thanksgiving.

I see the corn.

It is Thanksgiving.

I see the turkey.

It is Thanksgiving.

I see the pie.

It is Thanksgiving.

What do you see?

Key Words

corn

pie

table

turkey

yams

Index

About the Author

Pearl Markovics loves holidays of every kind—especially the ones that include sweets and lots of presents.

Teaching Tips

Before Reading

- ✔ Guide readers on a "picture walk" through the text by asking them to name the things shown.

- ✔ Discuss book structure by showing children where text will appear consistently on pages.

- ✔ Highlight the supportive pattern of the book. Note the consistent number of sentences and words found on each page.

During Reading

- ✔ Encourage children to "read with your finger" and point to each word as it is read. Stop periodically to ask readers to point to a specific word in the text.

- ✔ Reading strategies: When encountering unknown words, prompt readers with encouraging cues, such as:

  - **Does that word look like a word you already know?**
  - **It could be _____ , but look at _____ .**
  - **Check the picture.**

After Reading

- ✔ Write the key words on index cards.

  - **Have readers match them to pictures in the book.**
  - **Have children sort words by category (words that start with *t*, for example) or food type.**

- ✔ Encourage readers to talk about other holidays.

- ✔ Ask readers to identify their favorite page in the book. Have them read that page aloud.

- ✔ Ask children to write their own sentences about a holiday. Encourage them to use the same pattern found in the book as a model for their writing.

Credits: Cover, © Sayers1/Shutterstock; 1, © mphillips007/iStock; 2–3, © YinYang/iStock; 4–5, © tobkatrina/Shutterstock; 6–7, © Andi Berger/Shutterstock; 8–9, © robynmac/iStock; 10–11, © Stephen Mcsweeny/Shutterstock; 12–13, © J-Roman/iStock; 14–15, © Monkey Business Images/Shutterstock; 16T (L to R), © robynmac/iStock and © J-Roman/iStock; 16B (L to R), © Spiderplay/iStock, © Stephen Mcsweeny/Shutterstock, and © Andi Berger/Shutterstock.

Publisher: Kenn Goin   **Senior Editor**: Joyce Tavolacci   **Creative Director**: Spencer Brinker

Library of Congress Cataloging-in-Publication Data in process at time of publication (2019)
Library of Congress Control Number: 2018023810
ISBN-13: 978-1-64280-115-6 (library binding) | ISBN-13: 978-1-64280-150-7 (paperback)

10 9 8 7 6 5 4 3 2 1